West Chicago Public Library District
118 West Washington
West Chicago, IL 60185-2803
Phone # (630) 231-1552
Fax # (630) 231-1709

abdobooks.com

Published by Magic Wagon, a division of ABDO, PO Box 398166, Minneapolis, Minnesota 55439. Copyright © 2021 by Abdo Consulting Group, Inc. International copyrights reserved in all countries. No part of this book may be reproduced in any form without written permission from the publisher. Claw™ is a trademark and logo of Magic Wagon.

Printed in the United States of America, North Mankato, Minnesota.
082020
012021

 THIS BOOK CONTAINS RECYCLED MATERIALS

Written by Bailey J. Russell
Illustrated by Neil Evans
Edited by Tamara L. Britton
Art Direction by Victoria Bates

Library of Congress Control Number: 2020930104

Publisher's Cataloging-in-Publication Data

Names: Russell, Bailey J., author. | Evans, Neil, illustrator.
Title: The portal / by Bailey J. Russell ; illustrated by Neil Evans.
Description: Minneapolis, Minnesota : Magic Wagon, 2021. | Series: The haunting of Hawthorne Harbor; book 3
Summary: The Portal is wide open and the Seers are busy taking care of ghosts. Mary visits the Portal every day looking for her brother. A ghost that looks like Paul steps through but it is not him. Who is this ghost, and why can't Mary bring herself to take care of him?
Identifiers: ISBN 9781532138386 (lib. bdg.) | ISBN 9781532139109 (ebook) | ISBN 9781532139468 (Read-to-Me ebook)
Subjects: LCSH: High school students--Juvenile fiction. | Ghosts--Juvenile fiction. | Brothers and sisters--Juvenile fiction. | Mistaken identity--Juvenile fiction. | Supernatural--Juvenile fiction. | Mystery and detective stories--Juvenile fiction.
Classification: DDC [FIC]--dc23

Table of CONTENTS

CHAPTER ONE	4
CHAPTER TWO	15
CHAPTER THREE	28
CHAPTER FOUR	39
CHAPTER FIVE	50
CHAPTER SIX	60
CHAPTER SEVEN	73
CHAPTER EIGHT	84
CHAPTER NINE	94
CHAPTER TEN	103

Chapter ONE

Mary wore black gloves to Paul's funeral. They itched. She picked at one of the cuffs while she sat in the front pew, waiting for the last few people to leave. It was stuffy in the small church, and someone had opened a window. Outside the rain fell—a constant hush through the trees.

The wooden pew was hard, and her left leg started to go numb. Mary uncrossed her legs and stretched them out in front of her, rolling her ankles first to the right, then to the left. Her black tights made her shins look shiny, and her dress was too short, but it was the only black one she had with pockets.

A little girl sat playing jacks at the front of the church, just a few feet from Mary.

The girl had blond hair tied up in bows, and snowman-patterned pajamas. During the entire service, she had bounced the ball on the hardwood floor and then scooped up four or five silver jacks at a time. Over and over again. Every now and then she would look up at Mary and yawn, blinking her eyes slowly, like a kitten. Whenever she yawned, Mary had to yawn too.

Mary wondered if the little girl knew she was dead. She hoped not. That was probably the worst—to actually know that you're a ghost and that your body is somewhere rotting in the ground.

The little girl bounced the ball again. This time it rolled away from her. Mary bent down and picked up the ball, holding it out for the girl. To anyone else, it would have appeared as if Mary was just looking at her own empty palm.

When the girl stood up and faced Mary, it was easier to see the bruising around the girl's neck and the dark pattern where her shattered cheekbone was slightly sunken in.

When she first saw the girl, Mary had instantly recognized her from the newspaper, though she had forgotten her name. Four years earlier, just after Christmas, the six-year-old girl was found dead in her parents' backyard. She was strangled and beaten, with a broken leg, the back of her head bashed in. There was nothing to indicate that the parents had been involved in their daughter's death. There were no other suspects or leads, and the case was never solved.

Instead of giving the ball back, Mary placed her other hand on top of the girl's head. Even through the silk glove Mary could feel the blood oozing from the back of the child's head. She closed her eyes, drawing in a

deep breath. Mary pictured a dandelion gone to seed—a hundred stars forming their own perfectly round galaxy. She held the flower up to her lips, then blew. The stars scattered in all directions, dissolving across the sky. Mary opened her eyes and the girl was gone.

Since the Portal had opened five weeks earlier, Mary had personally taken care of more than thirty ghosts. She was talented, even Abby agreed. It had come easily to Mary after the first terrifying attempt in the burning gym. But it wasn't something she got used to. Children were the hardest.

Mary brushed off her hands, even though there was nothing on them. Her parents were still talking to the funeral director. She could just hear the soft flow of their voices from where they stood by the front door, but not actual words.

An abandoned funeral pamphlet lay on the

pew beside her. Paul's face was on the cover. Their mother had chosen his senior picture. In it he had a toothy, open-mouthed smile. Paul hadn't liked that picture, but Mary did.

For the thousandth time, Mary wondered why her brother's ghost hadn't come back. What did it take? Didn't slamming your car into a tree qualify as having unresolved issues? But Dan had said that there might not be any reason to it. The legend that ghosts still had work left to do on earth before they could "move on" might be all wrong. And shouldn't she wish that her brother was at peace?

Mary took out her phone. No messages. She kind of hoped that Dan had sent her something. Even just a quick "hi." Chloe and James had come to the funeral, but she didn't invite Tom, Abby, or Dan. Part of her worried that if they were at the church and her brother's ghost appeared, they might take care of Paul before she had a chance to talk to him.

She wondered what Dan was doing. He had missed a lot of school after the fire. To be honest everyone had. They shut the whole school down for two weeks while they investigated how the fire started. It had rained the entire time.

September was sometimes beautiful in Hawthorne Harbor: day after day of blue sky before fall settled in for good and brought dead leaves and a constant drizzle. Not this year. It was as though the sky itself was mourning the two dead students. Cassandra Decker. Sean Howard. A senior and a junior—dead from third-degree burns and smoke inhalation.

Although the authorities never found a source for the fire, everyone blamed the senior prank. The most surprising part of the fire was how quickly it was put out and how little damage was actually done to the school. Just like the kitchen fire, there had been a lot of smoke damage, but the structure itself was mostly unharmed.

Mr. Flynn was fired, and then he immediately left town. He didn't even sell his house first. They needed to blame someone, and it was Mr. Flynn who had argued that they go ahead with the Lock-In, even after the lunch lady died.

Mary sometimes wondered if Mr. Flynn really did have something to do with it and had been working with Jane all along. But short of tracking down Mr. Flynn and questioning him, as Abby had suggested more than once—and she always held up air quotes when she said "question"—they really had no way to find out. Jane, after all, was gone for good.

When the service ended at ten thirty, Mary was supposed to go with her mom and dad and have brunch with her grandparents. Paul would have rolled his eyes at the idea of a funeral brunch. He thought brunch was for women who wanted to sit around and gossip.

Mary stood by her mom for a few minutes. She was speaking to the funeral director about the flowers. She wanted to donate them to the hospital.

"Give them to a new mother. Fill her room with flowers." Her mom's voice shook as she spoke, and she still held that box of tissues, slightly crushing it with her grip.

Her mom was a few inches taller than Mary, with dyed brown hair. It had gone mostly gray when she was only twenty-three. Mary had recently begun staring at her own roots in the mirror, searching for strands of silver.

The funeral director nodded. "Of course, Mrs. Paine. That's a lovely idea."

"It's what Paul would have wanted," her mom said, dabbing her eyes.

Mary almost snorted at the idea of Paul ever having a single thought about the disposal of a room full of white lilies. The flowers were very strong smelling and were starting to make Mary's eyes water. What new mother would want death flowers in her room?

Mary's dad stood beside his wife but didn't say anything. He had a lost expression and patches of stubble on his throat that he had overlooked while shaving that morning. He looked like someone who had just woken up on a bus and hadn't yet figured out that he'd missed his stop.

Finally, Mary gave a little *I'm leaving* wave. She put on her coat in the lobby and walked out the front door. She would text her mom a little later and tell her that she went over to Chloe's. The thought of sitting through brunch with her weepy grandparents made her feel nauseous. They were staying another night, so she'd see them at dinner.

Chapter Two

Abby was driving, which meant that when she came to a stop sign on the way out of town the car lurched and stalled. "C'mon," Abby muttered, grinding the stick into first gear. The car stuttered when she stepped on the gas, almost dying again. James's seat belt tightened across his chest as he was jerked back and forth. Tom groaned from the seat behind Abby.

Dan didn't say anything, for once, because he wasn't there. He had stayed home because his shoulder was still healing. James didn't miss Dan's lectures, or the way he squinted his eyes disapprovingly whenever James spoke. Plus, it was Dan's car, and listening to Abby brutalize his transmission would probably

have given him an aneurysm.

The car finally sped forward, skidding for a moment on the wet road. "You drive like a psycho," Tom said, kicking the back of Abby's seat.

"Can you work a stick?" James asked Tom. Tom laughed like James had made a joke, and Abby snorted.

"Sure," Tom answered. "I'm a pro."

James turned back to Abby and asked, "Then why don't you know how?" Abby was wearing her hair up, and he noticed a tiny mole on the side of her neck, just above her collarbone.

"It's not like we're Siamese twins," Abby replied. "His boyfriend taught him."

"Oh." James didn't realize Tom was gay. James tried to think of anything he might have said in the past few weeks that would have made him sound like a homophobic jerk. He didn't think he was a homophobic jerk, but who knew what might have spilled out of his mouth.

James glanced in the back seat. Tom gave him a cool, even smile, like he was daring James to have a problem with this new information. In middle school, James used to say that things were "gay"—like, taking a head shot in Halo was gay. His mom would yell at him when he talked like that.

"You have a boyfriend?" James asked.

"Nah," Tom said. "We broke up before we moved here. He's still in Texas."

"He was good looking," Abby said, turning up the wipers. The wipers made an annoying squeaking sound every time they swung to the right. *Squeak, thump, squeak, thump.*

The rain was getting heavier and the view out James's window was wet and gray. Everything outside of Hawthorne Harbor was crazy rural—like, cows and horses and little farmhouses. The road stretched up a long valley with wide pastures on either side. If it kept raining like this, the pastures would flood and it would look like you were driving up the middle of a huge, flat lake.

"He was alright," Tom said. "Kind of clingy, actually."

James didn't want to talk about Tom's ex-boyfriend. He wanted to know what they were going to find at the lake about twenty miles out of town. He started punching at Dan's radio presets. Static. Had Dan really not set up his presets since moving to town? Weirdo.

"Here." Abby pressed the CD button. U2's "With or Without You" filled the car.

"No!" Tom yelled, covering his ears. "No more *Joshua Tree!*"

"I like it," Abby replied, turning the volume up even louder. She sang along, but James couldn't really make out her voice over the sound of the car wheels on the wet road, the squeaking windshield wipers, and the music coming from the tinny speakers.

When James had knocked on Abby's door that morning and told her about the old ghost story, he was about eighty percent sure that she would tell him not to waste her time.

A man had murdered his wife with an ax, dumped her body in the lake, and hung himself from the rafters of a boathouse. Sometimes the man's ghost came back and drowned people. When he told her the story, Abby's eyes had lit up and she said, "When do we leave?"

James had responded with, "How about right now?" because he needed to do something after sitting through Paul's funeral. He had been able to see the back of Mary's head during the service, but not her face. She probably didn't even know he was there. And Chloe had been a mess, with tears running down her unusually makeup-free face. The whole thing had made James restless and jumpy.

Abby was driving smoothly now that she could hang out in fifth gear. Pasture eventually gave way to trees. The road was so dark it seemed like late afternoon instead of morning. It was hard to believe that the whole day was still ahead of them.

The service had seemed to go on forever, and trying not to cry was exhausting. James felt bad for leaving right after the funeral, but Mary probably had family stuff to do. And, to be honest, he hated that church. It was the same one his mom had chosen when she planned her own funeral. He wondered if his mom had gone to her funeral, and if so, was she disappointed?

"Turn here!" James yelled over the music, pointing to a small road that peeled off to the left. He braced himself for Abby to take the turn too quickly, or kill the car, but she slowed and let the car gently roll onto the dirt road.

Tom leaned forward. "Good job!" he yelled in his sister's ear. "I didn't even throw up."

The road was in bad shape, with huge rain-filled potholes making the car tip to one side or almost bottom out. James felt like he was in a leaking boat. The windows had started to fog up, so James rolled down his window and stuck his hand out. He touched the dripping cedar branches as they passed.

"Now it's raining inside," Tom grumbled. "Wonderful." Ever since Abby had woken her brother up to come on their little adventure, Tom had been less than enthusiastic about the whole thing.

"Just stay on the road. It goes all the way to the lake," James yelled over the music. Abby nodded, tapping the steering wheel with her fingertips.

James had never met anyone like Abigail Moore before—at least outside of a movie. Mary always said she hated those characters: the ones who acted all crazy but were so hot the male characters fall in love with them immediately. The kind of girl who takes off her clothes and jumps in a fountain or hops on a train without knowing where it's going.

Mary used to go on rants that those girls weren't real. They were some Hollywood screenwriter's dream girl. James thought that Mary would probably have hated Abby if she were in a movie. Heck, Mary probably kind of hated Abby in real life. Mary always acted weird around her—nervous or something.

After four more teeth-rattling miles, they

arrived at Horseshoe Lake. Abby pulled off to the side of the road—there wasn't really much of a parking area—and turned off the car. The sudden silence made James's ears fuzzy, like they were full of cotton.

The lake was named after its shape: wide and narrow with a horseshoe-like curve and a narrow piece of land that jutted out into the middle of the water. At the end of this little peninsula was an old, rotting boathouse.

Fir trees and cedars surrounded the lake, making it feel like you were miles and miles from anything. They were miles from anything. James was pretty sure that no one would be able to hear them scream.

While he didn't really think that they'd find anything here, just thinking of the possibility gave him a pleasant chill down his spine, like watching a scary movie. Those were always his favorite kind.

The rain had eased up in the last few minutes. Rather than falling, it looked like the rain was just hovering in place as a thick mist.

"Okay . . . what's the plan?" Abby asked, looking back at her brother. James was a little annoyed that she obviously didn't direct the question toward him. Maybe James had an amazing plan. She didn't know. He didn't have a plan beyond driving to the lake, but he could have.

Tom looked out through the fogged glass. "I think I've seen this one before. We split up, right? One of us checks out the creepy shack. Someone else goes swimming—and maybe James wanders around the woods for a while until someone stabs him in the throat?"

Abby ignored her brother and turned to James. "I actually do think we should start with the building. Ghosts tend to stay in one place—somewhere they feel comfortable and safe. If there is a ghost here, I bet he'd want to be inside the shack."

"Boathouse," James corrected, then blushed. "I mean, yeah. Okay, sure." Over the past few weeks James had instituted a policy of agreeing with whatever Abby said.

As he got out of the car, he suddenly wondered how Mary was doing. She popped into his head all the time. This time, it wasn't just Mary in general that he thought about, but specifically "Mary in his basement"—that afternoon at the beginning of summer.

The memory of that afternoon was always with him. It stuck with him like a sticky, shameful film that clung to his skin. He thought about it all the time. Not the kiss exactly, but the look on her face. It wasn't just anger and it wasn't just pity—though he saw that her face was also full of both of those emotions. What he had seen in her eyes when he had tried to kiss her was worse. It was disappointment.

Chapter THREE

Dan's house wasn't that far from the church—maybe ten blocks. Mary didn't have an umbrella, but the rain felt nice on her face. It was like walking through a cloud.

On the way to Dan's she saw three more ghosts. The first was a middle-aged man who kept stepping out into the street and covering his head with his arms. Then he would vanish. He did this two times before Mary took care of him. Mary didn't even need to touch him. She just closed her eyes and imagined the man's body melting with the rain.

The second was another child. He sat on the sidewalk and looked up at Mary as she walked by. She might not have even known he was dead except for his hair—it wasn't wet, even in the rain. And his clothes looked old, like something you would see in a museum. Lace-up boots and a wool coat with wooden buttons.

At a quick glance Mary couldn't tell what had killed him. He just sat with his chin in his hands and watched her walk by. When she tried to place her hand on his head, it just passed right through. She snatched her hand back as the boy frowned up at her.

Some of the ghosts were stronger than others—that was something Mary had learned in the past five weeks. The little girl in the church had been strong. Mary could have picked her up and held her and rocked her. But she was still just an echo, and when Mary willed the girl's ghost to disperse, it had been easy. This boy was just a shadow. Mary didn't even have to touch him. It was even easier than the middle-aged man. Sometimes taking care of ghosts was like sweeping up cobwebs.

The third ghost was hiding behind a tree just a block from Dan's house. When she walked past, the ghost threw herself at Mary, pushing her down onto the sidewalk. Even though it all happened so fast, Mary recognized her. It was Angela Ivan.

Angela had been a friend of one of Paul's girlfriends. She had OD'd three years earlier. They found her body in the back seat of a car. Her friends had left her there to "sleep it off" and she had choked on her own vomit. The ghost had long, stringy blond hair and she smelled terrible—like decay. Angela snarled in Mary's ear. Then she was on Mary's back, still holding her by the hair. Mary struggled against the ghost, pushing herself up onto her hands and knees.

"Get off!" Mary hissed. Her knees stung

from hitting the pavement, and she was pretty sure her tights were ripped. They had cost twenty dollars. Now they were ruined.

Angela pulled Mary's head back and laughed. "I know you," she said in a singsong voice. "I know you."

Mary wanted to tell Angela that she didn't know anything about her. That she was only thirteen when Angela had died in the back of that old Toyota. But there was no point. Whomever the ghost thought she was, there was no talking her out of it. Ghosts were very single-minded.

Starting from the moment the ghost tackled her, it took Mary seven seconds to come up with a plan. She bet that Dan or Abby would have already had a plan before a ghost jumped them, but she was still learning. And Tom might have been able to talk his way out of it.

First, Mary let herself fall back onto her stomach. Her scalp screamed as she wrenched her head down too, taking Angela with her. Then, with Angela unbalanced, Mary reached up with both hands and grabbed her nasty hair. Mary's burned hands stung as she pulled the ghost's hair as hard as she could, flipping her over the top of her head. Angela landed hard on her back and let out a loud "oomph!" As if she had any breath in her lungs.

As fast as she could, Mary got to her knees and pulled her pocketknife out of her coat pocket. She flipped the knife open and slammed the blade into Angela's forehead. There wasn't any blood—that was the freaky part about stabbing a ghost. Angela rolled her eyes up toward the blade then let out a terrible scream. Mary covered her ears with her hands until the ghost disappeared.

Mary knelt in the rain for a few minutes

after the ghost vanished, waiting to see whether she was going to cry. Her eyes burned, but she blinked back the tears and breathed deeply until she was under control. Then she stood up slowly, wincing as she straightened her skinned knee.

The trickle of blood that ran down her leg looked worse than it really was because of the rain. Mary pressed one of her wet gloves to her knee and limped towards Dan's house. She hesitated when she got to the front door, then knocked.

It took a few tries before Dan opened the door. Mary's heart gave a little twist when she saw his sleep-rumpled hair and groggy eyes. "Hey," he said, blinking at her. "You're all wet." He was wearing a soft-looking white shirt and sweatpants. She must have woken him up.

"Yeah. It's raining."

He seemed to look past where she stood on the covered porch to the dripping lilac bush in the front yard. "Oh. You're right," he said.

Dan had been taking some serious pain meds as the hole in his shoulder slowly healed. He didn't like to talk about it, but Tom told Mary that the bullet had caused some nerve damage. Even if the actual wound was getting better, there was some pain that might never go away completely.

Mary was getting used to Dan's spaced-out, glossy eyes, but she didn't like it. She had come to rely on him, out of all of them, to know what was going on.

Mary walked past Dan and went straight to the kitchen. She grabbed a paper towel to clean up her bloody leg. Then she took the knife out of her pocket and dropped it on the table. Dan startled at the sound then crossed his arms.

"Four," Mary said. "I just took out four ghosts." She took off her coat and dropped it on a chair. "One in the church and three on the way here."

"I'm sorry," Dan said. He was always apologizing to her lately, like he was somehow to blame for everything. He had said he was sorry the other day when Mary spilled coffee on herself. Dan sometimes even apologized for the rain.

"I just . . ." Mary ran her hands through her wet hair. Her scalp was still tender from Angela's attack. "When's it going to end? Is this just the way the world is now? Like, forever? Just ghosts and more ghosts?"

Dan finally seemed to wake up enough to notice Mary's ripped tights and skinned knee. "You okay?"

Mary sighed. "No. I mean, yes. I'm fine. A vicious ghost pulled my hair and pushed me down. And I took care of her. But no. It's not fine. Can we just live like this? Is this what it's always like, in the places you were before? The other Portals?"

Dan got Mary a glass of water and one for himself. He drank deeply and rubbed his eyes again.

She knew he didn't like being medicated, which meant the pain must have been really bad today, because he was trying to cut down on the pills.

"No, none of the Portals were like this. We called them Portals, but they were more like doors. This one—it's wide open. I've never seen anything like it."

"Have you found anything?" she asked. Dan was supposed to be researching a way to close the Portal. So far, he had found a Web series about a cat who could fit in all kinds of boxes, and a Russian cartoon about a girl and her pet bear, but nothing about how to keep ghosts from flooding Mary's town.

Mary wasn't even sure how Dan was supposed to be researching—did he just Google "How to close a Portal to the Dead?" Maybe she should try that herself.

"Not really. Maybe. I don't know." Dan yawned. His breath wasn't great and Mary felt kind of bad for being annoyed that he wasn't finding answers. But she wasn't the one who got shot.

chapter FOUR

Mary still had dreams about it sometimes. In them, Dan is bleeding and she tries to help lift him but her burned hands hurt so bad she can't. Then the Portal keeps getting bigger and bigger until it swallows them both like an exploding sun. That is when she always wakes up—after it is too late, but before she actually can see what is on the other side.

Dan held his hand out to Mary. "Come on, I want to show you something."

He led Mary up the stairs to his room. They usually sat around the kitchen table when they talked, and Tom and Abby always took up all the space in the room with their bickering.

"Hey, where are the twins?" Mary asked.

Dan glanced back at her. "They ran off somewhere with James. They left about twenty minutes ago. He had a ghost he wanted to show them."

Mary could hear a slight twinge of bitterness in Dan's voice. She had grown used to Dan being a kind of ringleader for the trio. He couldn't enjoy being left behind. It was probably worse since they had gone off with James.

James must have come here right after the funeral. She didn't remember James or Chloe leaving, but she did recall seeing them near the back of the church with their families. She had spent most of the actual service watching the ghost of the girl, fascinated by the bows in her hair and how focused she was on her game of jacks.

"James has a ghost?" Mary sat on the edge of Dan's bed, her stomach doing a silly little flip as the mattress sank beneath her. Was it stupid to be shy about sitting on a boy's bed when she had just stabbed a ghost in the forehead?

Dan sat at the desk by the bed. He turned on his laptop. "You tell me. Something about a ghost by a lake? It drowns people?"

Mary had a vague memory about some ghost story James told her when they were both about ten years old. It was a man who drowned people or killed people with an ax. She had always thought James made it up. "Well, I'm pretty sure that all they'll find at Horseshoe Lake is water."

She looked around the room. The walls were bare and the room was fairly clean—clothes in a corner hamper, throw rug on the hardwood floor looking freshly vacuumed. His windows didn't have any curtains, and she could see out over the bluffs to the hazy line where the clouds met the water.

"Where'd you get this house?" Mary hadn't asked that before. She had wondered about it, though—how these kids who were her age could afford a giant Victorian house.

"What?" Dan glanced up from his computer. "Oh, it's Tom's. His and Abby's. They bought it."

"Bought it? Like, they own it? You're not renting? How is that possible?" Mary took in the walls around her, and the many rooms, and the roof that made up this great big house. It must have been worth a million dollars. Not that she really knew what houses cost—a million was always her go-to amount when anything was inconceivably expensive.

"Well, they don't actually like to talk about it. They have some money. From . . . a settlement."

"A settlement?"

"Um." Dan looked uncomfortable. He ran his hand through his hair and winced as he moved his shoulder. "I'll let them tell you. You can ask them about it when they get back."

"Sure." That was weird. She wondered what was going on with that. Mary looked down at her skinned knee. She poked a finger through her torn leggings to the drying blood. It hurt, but she kept doing it without thinking, like picking at a hangnail. "Anyway, you were going to show me something?"

"Yeah." Dan turned his laptop around towards her. The screen showed a news article about a serial killer in Arizona. A few years earlier someone had killed four women by slitting their throats, but he was never caught.

Mary just assumed the killer was a he. It happened right around Halloween, so they called the murderer the Halloween Killer.

Dan pointed at the article, actually pressing his finger on the screen. Mary hated when people did that. She wanted to wipe the fingerprint off the screen with the fabric of her dress, but she resisted.

"This town had a Portal too," Dan said. "But after these women died, it closed. I think the killings were a ritual."

"It says that?" Mary got up and leaned over his shoulder. "It mentions the Portal?"

"No, of course not. But we had it marked on the map as a Portal that just vanished. It's very odd for a Portal to disappear, so I remembered it."

Mary tried to make sense of this new information. They already knew that a Portal had closed before and didn't tell her? She considered this and decided to let that one go. There was so much she still didn't know about the trio.

"Okay," she said, "but now you think these murders had something to do with it?"

"Yeah. Slitting someone's throat is very ritualistic. Bloodletting, sacrifice . . . all that stuff. And they were all killed near the Portal."

Mary shook her head. "That doesn't make any sense. Why would Jane try to kill a ton of people to keep the Portal closed if she could have just killed four people to close it later? That doesn't sound very efficient."

"I don't think we'll ever know what was going on in her head. Or what happened in the last fire. Not unless Jane's ghost comes back for an interview. Maybe the fire was the only ritual she knew? She was obviously pretty scared about what would happen if the Portal opened."

Mary remembered Jane's face in the darkness—how devastated she looked when she knew she had failed. It was hard not to feel sorry for a terrified old woman, but Mary did her best. Just thinking about Jane made Mary clench her teeth so hard that her jaw hurt.

Mary sat back down on the bed. Leaning over Dan's shoulder was starting to get uncomfortable. The she realized what he was actually showing her. "Wait, so you do know how to close it?"

Dan nodded, smiling at her. Then he shook his head. "No. I mean, I don't. But someone might. If I'm right and these killings were part of a ritual..."

"Someone? Are there others like us? Other Seers?"

Dan rubbed his shoulder, looking back to the computer. "Not exactly like us, but yeah—other people know about the Portals. Other people can see ghosts. How do you think I learned anything?"

Mary frowned. "Yeah, I guess. I just didn't think there were chat rooms and stuff."

Dan yawned and put his hand over his shoulder again. His eyes drooped. "Sorry, what'd you say?" He looked terrible.

Mary really wanted to know more about those other people and this possible ritual, but Dan was obviously fading. He'd let her know when he found something useful. She just had to trust him. "Nothing. Come here." Mary got up and patted the now empty bed. "You should lie down. I'll go."

Dan lay down on the bed, but he took Mary's wrist before she could leave. "Wait," he said. His hand was warm and she could feel her pulse beating beneath his fingers.

Mary couldn't look him in the eye. "What?"

"Just . . . you can stay a little longer. If you want. You look tired, too." Dan scooted over so he was against the wall.

The bed was a twin, but there was just enough room for two people. She took off her shoes and lay down next to Dan.

chapter FIVE

"You smell nice," he said into her hair, his words slurring a little with sleep. She didn't say that her neck tingled where his breath touched her skin. Instead, she asked, "Where'd you grow up?"

He didn't answer right away. Mary started to think that he had fallen asleep because his breath was so even. She could feel his chest rise and fall against her back. Then, in a low whisper, he said, "I guess San Francisco. That's when I still lived with my parents."

"What was it like?" she asked, though what she really wanted to know was what had happened to his parents. What had happened to him? What had made him this way?

"We had a lemon tree in our backyard and

we lived at the top of a really big hill. San Francisco's supposed to be so foggy all the time, but I just remember that it was sunny. I remember lying on my back and looking up at the blue sky through the trees. I think it was somewhere in the Mission District, but I don't really know. I was seven."

Mary held her breath, as though any sound—any distraction—would make him stop.

"I don't know why my sister was out that night. She was fourteen. When I was seven that seemed so old. My parents should have known where she was. How could they not have known? It's like the one job a parent has—keep your child safe.

"But they didn't know where she was and they didn't realize when she didn't come home that night. Someone found her three days later in an alley.

"The police thought she had been dead for about twelve hours, which meant there were two full days when she was still alive—and whatever they did to her, she could still feel it. She knew it was happening." Dan took a deep, shaky breath, like he had just surfaced from beneath the water. He let it out slowly while Mary tried to figure out what to say.

"That's horrible." Mary took his hand, wincing at the pressure against the palm of her hand. She could feel the soft hair of his arm against the skin of her own arm.

"Yeah. I didn't really know what was happening at first. At seven, you actually realize a lot more than people think. I knew she was dead. I knew I'd never see her again. I knew what it meant when someone was murdered. But they tried to keep the worst of it from me. If my sister hadn't come back, I might never have known."

"You saw her? Her ghost?" Dan's fingers grazed her neck, and Mary tried not to shiver.

"She was the first ghost I ever saw. I thought I was dreaming because I knew she was dead. And dead people didn't ever come back to visit. My mom kept explaining that to me, like I wouldn't understand if she didn't keep telling me over and over again. She even compared it to when our dog Bowser was hit by a car. As if a dog in the road was at all the same as my sister."

"You actually had a dog named Bowser?" Mary winced at her question. Yeah, because that was the important part of the story.

"Nah. I don't remember his name. I'm sure it was clever though. A character out of a book or some mythological reference. My parents always thought they were so clever. Maybe it was Bowser. They would have actually loved that—thought it was ironic or something.

"Don't you sometimes wish that pets would come back instead of people? Puppies and hamsters following us around? Little kitten ghosts?"

Mary gave a little laugh, but she didn't want Dan to get sidetracked. And she actually thought that ghost pets would be a little creepy. She asked, "What happened? When you saw your sister, I mean?"

"She came to see me after I was tucked into bed. Like I said, at first I thought I was dreaming. She would talk to me like she was really there.

"But she didn't look right. It was her eyes, to start with. She wouldn't open her eyes. Estrella. That was her name. Stella. She would brush her cold hands across my face and kneel on the side of my bed. She would sing to me sometimes. Songs from the radio or lullabies our mom used to sing.

"She would always get upset if I talked to her, but I wanted to ask questions. Wasn't she dead? Was she a ghost? That kind of thing. She would put her hands over my mouth and shush me. It was always dark, so I didn't see the worst of it until one night when I got out of bed and pushed past her. I turned on the light.

"My sister's face had been cut. Long lines from the top of her forehead down to her chin. There was blood under her eyes and she wouldn't open them. Couldn't open them. She couldn't see, to know the light was on.

"That's something I still wonder about. Why couldn't her ghost see? Even if they cut out her eyes when she was alive why couldn't she see after she died? Isn't death supposed to be this great release? Isn't it supposed to free you from pain? From suffering? Why couldn't my sister see?"

"Oh, Dan." Mary had been biting her cheek. She made herself stop and ran her tongue over the skin inside her mouth. She could feel the rough imprint her teeth had left. It tasted like blood.

"I didn't know what I was doing. I saw her like that—all of it. The raw red lines on her wrists where she had been tied up. The cuts on her arms and legs. I didn't want to see her like that. I wanted her to go away.

"I closed my eyes, and I used the trick my dad had taught me, for when I was afraid of a monster in my room. I imagined that the monster was a snowman in the summer and it was melting. So I imagined my sister melting. And I felt it—you know what I mean. I felt her, in my head. And then she was gone. I took care of her."

Mary shook her head against the pillow. "You didn't know what you were doing. You wouldn't have . . . I know you didn't mean it."

"But the thing is, if she came back here today, and I know what I know now, I would still do it." Dan rolled over so he was lying on his back. His voice was getting softer and slower. "She didn't deserve to be that way. She couldn't even see me. And her face . . . I would do it again."

Mary shook her head. "I don't believe you." Once again Mary pictured her brother as he was in his senior picture, with his stupid smile and his hair brushed back off his forehead. Not as he was in the hospital. Never that.

When Dan didn't answer, Mary turned to look at him. His eyes were closed, and his arm was flung above his head at an awkward angle.

"Dan?" she whispered, but he didn't move. Mary sat up carefully, then leaned over him. She pressed her lips to the side of his mouth where his skin was darkened with stubble. Then she went down the creaky stairs and put on her coat. She put her knife in her pocket and walked out the front door into the rain.

Chapter Six

The boathouse looked like something out of a horror movie. Moss covered the decaying roof, and the sides were a grayish green. The door was missing, so the front looked like a huge, gaping mouth.

James had first read about the dead man in a newspaper that his dad left out on the coffee table. He was nine or ten and usually just grabbed the comics.

That day, however, the headline caught his attention: Four Bodies Found at Horseshoe Lake. They didn't include a picture of the man's body hanging from the low rafters of the boathouse, but they did have a picture of the lake—black and white and grainy.

Apparently, the fall wasn't enough to break

the man's neck, so he had probably strangled to death. The reporter had described the body: he was "severely decomposed." They found his wife's body in the shallows. Both had been dead for a few weeks.

James had imagined the woman's body surfacing, gray and leathery, like one of those manatees in the Everglades. James didn't actually know what a dead body looked like, but he knew exactly what a manatee looked like because they had studied them in fifth grade.

The strangest part of the article was the second couple. They had only been dead for a few days, and they were both drowned. No sign of a struggle—like they had each held their own heads under the water and breathed in the greenish, murky lake water that was contaminated with the decomposing body of the dead woman. Disgusting.

James had thought about that story for years, wondering what had actually happened. It was a mystery that the town wanted to forget. Hawthorne Harbor already had the Fire, the specters of the burned students looming over it. It didn't need a haunted lake as well. The man who hung himself and murdered his wife were both older people. They had no children and had lived outside of town in a crappy mobile home in the woods. They were easy to forget.

The drowned couple was younger, in their early twenties. Just out of college and traveling. A tragic accident, but they had no family nearby to miss them.

When James told Mary the story, he had tried to tell it the way he thought about it—the way he dreamed about it. That man climbing down from his rope and wading into the water. He must have pulled the man under the water first, James thought, and then the woman.

Abby walked faster than James, and he had to kind of half jog to keep up. "In a hurry?" he called to her.

"It's raining. I want to get this over with." But Abby was grinning. She slowed down a little and let James catch up. Tom had hardly moved from the car. He stood grimacing down at the sticky muck along the shore.

"Hurry up!" Abby yelled to her brother.

"This place smells terrible," Tom called back. "And yes, let's all just run into the haunted shed. Great idea."

When they reached the boathouse, they all peered in one of the broken windows. The building was big enough for two or three canoes or rowboats to fit side by side. But there weren't any boats there today. Just a bunch of trash and some broken beer bottles.

A few empty milk crates were off to one side.

"See anything?" James asked. He couldn't see anything ghostly himself.

Abby shook her head. "Nah, empty."

James didn't know why he couldn't see ghosts the way the others did. Dan had always said there were levels of sight, but James's level seemed like the ground floor. Mary could see things that even Dan couldn't, like that ghost with the goggles.

James couldn't even really see the Portal, just a sort of wavy, mirage-thing that would disappear if he looked at it straight on. And ghosts were usually completely invisible to him. But he had seen something like fire at school a few times.

That first day of school, when Mary had seen the ghost of a teacher burning, James had seen flames appear out of nowhere, licking the air around the front of the classroom for a few seconds before they vanished.

But ever since the Portal opened and the town was just flooded with ghosts, he couldn't really see anything. He would stare toward a ghost that the others said they could see and maybe he would see something that looked like heat haze rising off the cement—if he were lucky.

Once he felt a shiver of cold when he was walking down the street, and Mary told him he'd just passed through a ghost. James hated it. If someone had poured this "superpower" out of a bottle, then all James had gotten was the spit-filled backwash at the end.

They walked to the lake side of the boathouse. Tom was right—the lake did smell kind of nasty. James stepped in some green duck droppings and tried to wipe off his shoes on the patchy, wet grass. The smell reminded James of dead fish and rotting grass clippings left out too long in the yard.

Abby went into the boathouse first, holding a big flashlight over her head like she thought she was a cop from a movie.

"Cozy," Tom said, covering his nose with his sleeve. "We could summer here."

James gestured to the thick beams that ran along the ceiling. "He must have hung himself there."

Abby pointed the light to the rafters. They startled a small bird. It flapped its wings but didn't fly away. "I don't know. I'm just not feeling it." Spiderwebs caught the light, and James ducked lower to avoid them.

"Sorry," James mumbled. She shouldn't have been this disappointed. Did she actually want to find a murderous ghost? "I thought it was worth a look."

"No prob." Abby smiled at James. "I needed an excuse to practice driving a stick anyway."

Tom grabbed the flashlight out of Abby's hands. He held it up under his chin. "I vant to suck your bluuud!" He wasn't holding it right, so the beam of light went right into Abby's eyes.

"Idiot," Abby hissed. She turned and left the boathouse. James could never tell when Abby was going to laugh at something her brother did or get all irritated with him. She kind of scared him most of the time.

James went after her, catching up to her by the edge of the water. "So, what next?"

Abby picked up a twig and threw it into the lake. "How exactly does this ghost kill people? In the story?"

"Well, like I said, everyone drowned." After that first young couple died, three more people drowned in the lake. The drownings happened years apart and could easily have been accidents.

"One man was fishing by himself. When he was found he was floating in the lake beside his boat, along with several empty beer cans. The authorities thought it was pretty obvious he had died operating a motor vehicle while drunk.

"The two most recent deaths were another young couple. A woman and her boyfriend were visiting the area from Portland. Again, it was a case of drowning with no signs of a struggle. Nothing to suggest that it wasn't just a terrible accident."

"Well, I say we lure it out." Abby took off her raincoat and flung it at her brother who was still standing in the boathouse, out of the rain. Tom didn't make a move to catch it, and the coat fell into the lakeside muck. Abby rolled her eyes at her brother.

Then she took off her shirt.

James swallowed and looked down at his

feet. "What are you doing?"

"It's just a swimsuit." She slipped off her shoes, shimmied out of her jeans, and stood at the lake's edge in a very sporty black-and-blue two-piece. She reminded James of one of those Olympic beach volleyball players.

"Let's see if he takes the bait," Abby said. Then, before James could say anything, she ran into the water. She shrieked at the cold and laughed as she sucked in her breath.

"Hey!" Tom came out of the boathouse. "You know I was joking earlier? About you swimming? I know, it's kind of hard to tell when I'm joking since I'm usually so very serious."

"Water's great!" Abby called back to them. She was waist-deep, with her arms crossed over her chest. It had to be freezing. Abby was kind of far away to really tell, but James thought her lips were turning purple.

"Don't get swimmer's itch!" Tom yelled, while his sister called out, "Come on in!"

James's disappointment at not finding the ghost quickly vanished. He took off his shirt and shoes and then ran into the water, splashing his way to Abby.

"Whoa!" James yelped. The cold water hit him like a punch to the gut, sucking the breath out of him. Some kind of water weed was caught in Abby's hair. She looked like a mermaid, even in the murky water.

Tom stood on the shore and looked out at Abby and James. "You're both going to catch pneumonia and die, and then your ghosts are going to haunt me," he said. "I'll be the only one who can see you, but I'll ignore you. How'll you like that? It'll be like an episode of the *Twilight Zone*."

"Dan and Mary could see us!" James called back.

James dove under the freezing water, instantly regretting it as the lake water went up his nose. He sputtered back to the surface and looked to see whether Abby noticed him flailing around like an idiot. She wasn't there.

"Abby?" James called out. "Abby?"

"Abby!" Tom ran to the water's edge and threw himself into the water. He didn't even stop to take off his shoes. "Do you see her?"

James swung around wildly. They had gone out deeper before she vanished, and the water was about up to his chest . . . which meant that it was probably up to Abby's chin. She was pretty tall for a girl, but not as tall as him.

"I can't see her. I can't . . ." Then James saw some strands of red hair floating near the surface like algae. "There!" He and Tom swam towards her.

Tom was the better swimmer. He glided through the water like an otter and then went under. He tried to pull his sister up, but she was caught on something. There was violent thrashing beneath the surface of the lake. It reminded James of those nature videos of alligators, where they catch their prey in the water and spin and spin until they drown the victim.

"I see the ghost," Tom gasped when he came up to take a breath. "He has her feet. I'm going back down." He disappeared with another splash.

James stood perfectly still in the green water, his feet sinking slightly into the slimy muck. His nose still hurt from snorting in water, and he had no idea what to do. He waited for three heartbeats for the twins to come back to the surface. But they were just shadows struggling beneath the water.

It was pouring by then, and the rain pocked the surface of the lake. Taking a deep breath, James dove back under. He made himself open his eyes. They stung, and he could barely see through the silt that Tom and Abby were churning up. He was probably going to get eye worms or something.

James could just make out Abby's bare arms and legs, and he swam towards them. Tom had his hands under Abby's arms and was trying to pull her away from whatever had her legs. Abby was kicking and struggling, her face covered by a cloud of her long red hair.

James swam for Abby's feet. He wished he had a harpoon or a trident like Ariel's dad in *The Little Mermaid*. That's who Abby looked like—Ariel. Not that it mattered right now. What he needed was something pointy, like a long stick, so he could stab the ghost (that he couldn't even see) from a safe distance. But all he had were his hands.

What would Mary do? Several times she had tried to explain to James how she got rid of ghosts. Mary said that she let her mind take hold of them. She could feel what held them together, what kept them—their bodies?—from flying into a million little pieces. Then she pulled them apart. It made no sense to James, but he needed to try something.

James put his hands on Abby's jerking legs. They were slimy and kept slipping from his grip. He thought that if the ghost had a hold of Abby's legs, then he could find the ghost by running his hand down to her feet. It wasn't a good plan, but James had no other ideas at the moment.

Tom had gone up for another breath, and James could hear the muted sound of him yelling. He wondered what Tom was saying.

Abby had stopped kicking and seemed to float limply. Tom was still tugging on her

arms, but her legs were clearly being pulled down towards the mucky bottom. James tried grabbing at the area beneath Abby, but he only felt water and stringy weeds.

James tried pulling on Abby's legs himself, but she was stuck fast. He could feel his lungs aching. Soon he would need to take a breath.

He burst up, pushing his face up out of the water and sucking in air. Tom had his head above the water, still pulling on his sister.

"Do you see him?" James gasped, his mouth barely working.

"He's down there. I'm not strong enough. We need Dan." James could barely understand Tom through his chattering teeth. Tom's wet hair was plastered to his forehead, and his lips looked blue. James had never seen Thomas Moore like this—with eyes wide and terrified.

James took another deep breath. He dove

down again and nearly poked his eye out on an algae-covered branch. Perfect! He broke off the sharp end of the branch, cutting his palm in the process. It stung. Now he would probably have a hand infection and eye worms.

He tried to ignore the pain and focus on what he held in his hands. Now he had what he needed. A foot-long stabby thing. A spear.

The water around his face clouded even more with his own blood, and he could feel vomit coming up his nose. James stared at Abby's limp feet. He held his stinging, twitching eyes open, willing himself to see something—anything. He tried to be Mary, to think with her brain. What would she see?

Finally, he saw. Not a person exactly but a shimmery, greenish smudge. It could have been anything, maybe the light from the sun finally breaking through the rain clouds, or just a patch of different colored algae. But it wasn't. It was James's smudge. His ghost.

James put his hand on Abby's cold, slippery ankle and stabbed the water just below her foot. He imagined that he was popping a balloon and all the air was going to shoot out in a jet of bubbles. He imagined a great white shark tearing through a school of fish, making them scatter.

James thought he heard a scream, only it didn't sound muffled by the water. It was close and angry. It sounded like a man. Then Abby's foot slipped through his hand. When James resurfaced, he saw Tom holding Abby against his chest, swimming them both to shore.

Abby had been under the water for two minutes and fifty-eight seconds. It had felt like an hour to James, but Tom had started counting the moment his sister's head vanished beneath the lake. He told this to James on the drive home, while Abby lay in the back seat with her head on Tom's lap, shivering and wrapped in the extra blankets that Dan kept in the trunk of his car.

When Tom first pulled his sister onto the shore, Abby wasn't breathing. James was about to start CPR. But Tom pushed him aside. He turned Abby onto her side and pounded on her back until lake water poured out of her mouth and nose.

She coughed and coughed, curled around herself. James would never have said it out loud, but with greenish slime sticking to her chin, Abby looked like something that had already started to decompose.

"You stupid . . ." Tom murmured, lying down and wrapping himself around her. Abby coughed some more, hacking and spitting out more lake muck. Then she turned to James and grinned a freaky, teeth-chattering grin. "Did it work?"

"What?" James was on his hands and knees in front her, ready to do something—anything—if she needed him.

"Did you get him?" Abby's freckles stood out on her bloodless face. She tried to lift a hand, probably to brush her hair out of her eyes, but Tom had pinned her arms to her side in his embrace. James moved the strand of hair for her.

"Yeah. I think so." James felt himself grin too, though his face was almost too numb to feel it.

Tom glared at him. "Your first ghost." With Tom's face mostly buried in the back of Abby's neck, James could barely hear him. "You two. I make the plans from now on."

Abby coughed, spit out more lake water, then struggled against her brother until he helped her sit up. "So," Abby said between coughs. "When are we ... doing this ... again?"

chapter EIGHT

After Mary left Dan's house she went straight to the Portal. Mary didn't really plan it, she just started walking. Today wasn't just Paul's funeral. It was his birthday. He would have been nineteen today, and he would have been away at college. She wouldn't have even seen him today if he were still alive. Paul didn't like to talk on the phone, but she still could have called him and sung the happy birthday song in the chipmunk voice that she always did to make him laugh.

The University of Washington wasn't that far—she and her parents might have taken the ferry to Seattle for the day and gone out to dinner with Paul. They could have gotten Indian food because that was Paul's favorite.

Or she and all her friends might be dead. Because if Paul hadn't died, Mary wouldn't be able to see ghosts. She wouldn't have been able to stop Jane from burning down the school. Maybe Dan could have done it—but he never actually saw the ghost that started the fires. Mary often wondered why she was the only one who could see the man in the goggles.

Mary could get to the Portal from the school grounds, but she preferred to go a few blocks past the school and take a little path through the woods. That way she didn't have to climb over the fence.

She wasn't the only one who walked around in the woods behind the school. There were lots of little paths back there, and you could even cut through the woods and take a trail down to the beach below. It was quite steep, though, and wasn't really an official trail.

When it was wet it was pretty dangerous.

Once Mary had taken the wrong path back there and found an old La-Z-Boy recliner someone had hauled into the woods. It was soaked from the rain and had a big rip along the headrest. Mary wasn't sure if this was an alternative to hauling it to the dump or if someone actually sat in it from time to time.

It only took a few minutes from the road using the path. She had been there so many times that her feet knew the steps by heart. When she got to the Portal, Mary stopped and crouched down among the blackberry vines. They caught on her tights, tearing more long runs in the black fabric.

Rain dripped off the edge of her hood and splattered onto her knee. She shivered, watching the light from the Portal throb and flicker. It was almost beautiful, but it was also terrible.

Almost every single day since the Portal opened, Mary had come here and watched the ghosts come through. At first, they came out quickly—shadows that seemed to stretch their way out like blobs in a lava lamp. They would press against the Portal, and the pulsing light would bulge and bend outward until they broke through.

It was almost like the ghosts were being born. That's how Mary had tried to explain it to James because he couldn't see it the way she could. He said that if he squinted and looked out of the corner of his eye he could see a glimmer. That was all.

Once the ghosts broke free, they tended to do one of several things. Some of them ran—fleeing through trees and brambles and off into the distance. Others just vanished. Mary wondered where they went. Could ghosts wish themselves back to the houses they had

lived in when they were alive or to a favorite coffee shop? Or maybe it wasn't a place. Perhaps they wished themselves close to the one they loved when they were alive.

Or maybe they simply dissolved like the burned lunch lady. When she realized she was dead, it looked like she had just faded away. Dan said she wasn't one of the ghosts that lingered, but where did she go? Did the ghosts who vanished right after they died just go to the other side of the Portal? Could they still come back?

Some ghosts stopped once they came through the Portal. They looked around with bewildered expressions, like sleepwalkers who had just awoken and found themselves far from their beds. Mary took care of these ghosts. It wasn't hard—they scattered as soon as Mary imagined a dry leaf crumbling in her hand, or a sand castle melting in the waves.

Today, as she stared into the glow of the Portal and watched it waver and billow like a sheet caught in the wind, Mary wondered if it went the other way. Could a living person go through the Portal? What would happen? Would you become a ghost yourself? Mary wondered about this every time she came here. Could you actually go into that mysterious place?

This time, as she thought about what lay on the other side of the Portal, Mary decided to try something. She reached into her pocket and took out a quarter. She pressed her thumb against the dead president's face and ran her fingernail along the edge. Then she threw it at the Portal.

Light rippled as the quarter passed through, and the Portal seemed to bend inward. There was a strange smell, like burning plastic or hair. Then the coin was gone. Mary got up and looked on the other side of the Portal, but even if the quarter had passed through to the other side and back out into the woods, it would be nearly impossible to find in the dead leaves and blackberry vines.

Mary got down on her hands and knees and felt with the palms of her hands, but she couldn't feel the quarter. Part of her—a very small part—wanted to run into the Portal and see what would happen. It didn't mean she was going to do it. But she couldn't help what thoughts went through her head.

As she searched for the coin, the Portal began to move. Ghosts always came out of the side closest to the school. Mary was crouched on the other side, still feeling around for the quarter. As the Portal bulged away from her, she froze.

She had never witnessed a ghost coming out of the Portal from the other side before.

The Portal was slightly see-through, and she watched the trees distort and ripple on the other side.

Mary pulled her knife out of her coat pocket and opened it. When she had to stab a ghost to focus her energy, she'd always done it up close—actually pushing the blade into the ghost. She'd never thrown it before, and she wondered whether that was even possible.

Could you take care of a ghost by throwing a knife at it or by shooting it with a gun? Or did a person's hand have to be touching the weapon for it to work? Mary had a lot of questions about ghost combat and ghosts in general, but Dan didn't always have enough answers.

When the ghost stepped through the Portal, she could see enough to tell that it was a guy. He looked so familiar—tall, with thick hair. Something about the shape of his shoulders made her cry out, "Paul?"

She bit her cheek where it was already bloody and ragged. That was so stupid, saying Paul's name. But when he turned and looked at her through the wall of light, she was so certain. This was what Mary had been waiting for—the reason she had come here all those mornings and sat in the rain. Why she came alone. So she would be ready when Paul came back.

Chapter Nine

"Paul!" Mary called out again, this time on purpose. Her hood was making her feel claustrophobic so she threw it off, letting the water that dripped off the trees run down her face. The ghost just stood there, watching her.

Mary started to slowly walk to that side of the Portal, stepping gently on the brambles and soggy leaves. *Paul, please,* she thought. She wondered what she would see. Would he look like he did in the hospital? Or would he look like himself?

When Mary first saw her brother after the accident, she was so sure that it wasn't him. His face was red and puffy. His forehead was lumpy and looked as shiny and purple as an eggplant—so swollen that Mary thought it might split open as she stood there, trying not to scream. *Not him, not him, not him.* Those were the words she kept saying over and over in her head. She could feel the words in her mouth—the muscles of her tongue trying, but failing, to say them aloud.

Now, as she took the few steps around the Portal, all Mary could think was *Let it be Paul, let it be Paul.* She was so sure that when she saw his light-brown hair—so like her own—and dark jeans, she almost threw her arms around the ghost.

But when she wiped the rain out of her eyes with the back of her wrist—the knife still clasped firmly in her hand—she knew she was wrong. It wasn't Paul. It was just another strange ghost that she'd have to kill.

Mary pulled her hood back up and inspected the ghost. He was very close to her brother's build—in between Dan and

James's heights, but broader. His hair was shorter than Paul's and was actually quite a bit darker. Almost black. She didn't know why she had thought his hair was Paul's color. She had just seen what she wanted to see, she supposed.

She couldn't tell what color the ghost's eyes were, but he was watching her. He tracked her movements as she took a final step and stood directly in front of him.

The ghost wore jeans and a plaid shirt with a few buttons open at the neck. He either looked very retro or had been dead for a few decades. It was hard to tell, since people were always wearing vintage stuff they found in thrift stores. There was something off about his clothes, though. She soon realized what it was—he wasn't wearing a coat. But the rain fell straight through him, so he probably didn't mind.

It had only been about thirty seconds since the ghost passed through the Portal. In that time he had only stood there, as though waiting for Mary to make a move.

Mary took a step toward the ghost and held out her hand. *Stupid, stupid*, said the inner voice that sounded a bit like Chloe. Mary wanted to know how strong he was—whether he was just an echo. Also, it was easier for her to take care of a ghost if she could lay her hands on him. With the hand not gripping her knife, Mary tried to touch the ghost's shoulder.

Her hand went right through the plaid fabric. Mary tried not to be disappointed because that would make her a crazy person. She shouldn't be disappointed that the ghost she was trying to destroy was weak and couldn't touch her. Even though she knew the ghost wasn't Paul, those few moments when she had thought it might be her brother had shaken her. A small, tiny part of her thought that maybe—if this ghost wasn't just an echo—it might mean that her brother could still come back. That he might still know her.

Mary took a step back and prepared to dissolve this young man. It should have been easy, like flicking the rain off the brim of her hood. He was only an echo. Mary closed her eyes and felt her mind latching into him, feeling for the edges of him—the outline of his being.

Sometimes this part felt strangely intimate, like she could feel the inside of the ghosts' heads, or like she was reaching her hand into their chests like that creepy dude from *Indiana Jones and the Temple of Doom* who had pulled out a guy's beating heart.

This time, as she reached out towards the ghost, it felt different. Instead of just catching a firm hold of the wispy edges of the ghost, Mary felt like something was pushing back at her—a pulsing that filled her concentration like a steady, beating heart.

She opened her eyes. The ghost was still watching her and his hand was raised. "Wait," he said. His voice was soft, like leaves rustling down an empty road. "Just wait a minute."

Mary's first instinct was not to wait but rather to plunge the knife into his neck. That's what smart girls did—girls who didn't end up murdered in a soggy, depressing patch of trees. But the ghost was just an echo. A shadow. He couldn't actually hurt her. So she waited.

While Mary stared at his throat, trying to decide what to do, she noticed that she could sort of see through the ghost. Earlier, when she was standing behind the Portal, Mary had been able to see the ghost through the pulsing curtain of the Portal. Now she could faintly see the Portal throb and ripple behind him. What if more ghosts came out of the Portal while she hesitated? What if there were too many and they swarmed her?

Mary knew she was stalling. She didn't want to kill this ghost, who was looking her in the eye and asking for mercy.

"Who are you?" she finally said.

He looked up, into the rain. Then he looked back at her. "I . . . I need to do something." He didn't answer her question. Had he even heard her? When the rain fell through the ghost, he flickered, like the TV did when her mom vacuumed too close to it.

The way he spoke to her, he didn't sound weak. Dan had told her stronger ghosts could carry on a conversation. But she had never met one. Even the man with the goggles that was strong enough to burn down a building hardly seemed to speak. But her hand had gone right through this boy. What was he?

Chapter TEN

She tried again. "What's your name?"

He blinked, as though trying to remember. Mary hoped that when she died she wouldn't come back. She didn't want to be a shadow. She didn't want to forget herself.

"John," he said at last. His voice was getting louder, more real sounding. "John Hawthorne."

"Hawthorne?" Mary brushed the rain out of her face again, almost stabbing herself in the cheek. She put the knife back in her pocket, knowing she could get it back out and open in less than three seconds if she needed to. James had timed her.

He paused, raising one hand to his collarbone. Mary didn't know whether he even realized he was doing it. "Yes. Yes, that's my name. John Hawthorne." He shook his head. "I'm really here? It feels so . . . foggy. I can see you, but it's like you're down a tunnel or something." He took a step closer. "Too far away. Do I know you?"

"No." Mary took a step back. Her heel hit a rotting log, and she almost tripped. "You're dead. You know that, right?"

He blinked, then rubbed his face. "I guess. I mean, yeah . . . I know. I died, and then I was . . . somewhere else. For a long time. I'm not sure where that was. I was waiting for something, you know? Like I had a test to take or I had a doctor's appointment. But I just kept waiting."

Stab him! her Chloe-voice said. It also sounded a bit like James. *This isn't a meet-and-greet!*

"You have to hide," she heard herself say.

The ghost's eyes widened. "Why?" He let his hands fall to his sides. "What do I have to hide from?"

Mary couldn't see anything wrong with him. No bruises, no broken bones. His face was pale with dark eyebrows and a small, delicate nose. He would have been cute if he were alive. One of those brooding boys in movies who think really deep thoughts and pine for things.

Mary shook her head in reply, but she didn't really know what she would do yet. She should just do it—get rid of him so she wouldn't have to think about it anymore. But he just didn't look dead. And he was talking to her.

"I have to do something," the ghost—John—continued. "I have to stop something. It's why I died—I don't remember all of it, but I remember pieces of it. I remember running.

I remember I was running and there wasn't enough time and I needed to find something. There was something I had to do, and I ran out of time. Then I died. I think . . . I think it was terrible. I think I was afraid." He spoke in a rush, but also in a kind of matter-of-fact tone, like he was just reading from a list of things to do today.

"Do you remember how you died?" Mary asked. She shivered and folded her arms across her chest. She could feel her heart beating in her throat.

"No. I remember that I was alive . . . and then I wasn't. I just . . . I wasn't . . . anymore."

You burned to death fifty years ago, Mary almost said, but she held her tongue. What if ghosts really were like sleepwalkers? You weren't supposed to wake a sleepwalker, right? Maybe you weren't supposed to tell a ghost how he died.

She remembered the story of John Hawthorne, but when she first saw the ghost she hadn't connected him to the picture she'd seen at the school. Principal Hawthorne standing next to his nephew, his arm around the young man. It was up in one of the glass cabinets in the school hallway, next to some old trophies.

But if they had both died as the building collapsed, why did John look so perfect? Why didn't he look like how he died, like the little broken girl from the church? Like Dan's sister? Why wasn't he crushed or burned? Did that mean that Paul could be okay when he came back? Could he be normal?

Mary tried to think of a question to ask him—something that would help her decide what to do. Finally, she asked, "What do you want?"

John flickered again, the light of the Portal

pulsing behind him. "I want . . ." He rubbed his face again, like he was exhausted. Could a ghost even feel his own skin? "I just want to remember. I just want more time."

"You're not supposed to be here," Mary whispered.

"I know." He turned his green eyes to her. At least, she thought they were green. It was hard to tell in the shadows, and with the light of the Portal behind him. "I . . . I think I used to be like you. I think I used to know what ghosts were. What I am. I'm a ghost." He frowned and looked down at his shoes. "How strange."

He looked back at Mary. "I just need to remember. It's important. I need to do something, then I'll go. I just need a little more time. To remember." Mary hadn't said that she was going to make him . . . go away. Kill him. She hadn't said those words. But he seemed to know. Mary could hear the pleading in his voice. He was asking her permission. He was asking her for more time.

Time. Could Mary give him time? Was that something a person had the power to give? She thought about Paul, and how his birthday meant nothing now. He had no more time.

"Okay," Mary said. "Tomorrow. I'll come back tomorrow." John was just another echo, like the girl in the church or that woman in the movie theater. He was harmless. John couldn't even touch her. What could he do in one day?

"A day," John said, looking up to the tops of the trees. "It's been years, hasn't it? I didn't recognize it at first, but this is where the school was. It burned, didn't it?"

"Yes." Mary watched him, wondering how he'd react. He seemed so calm. "I'm sorry. You've been dead for . . . um . . . fifty years."

He nodded, like he'd expected her to say that. "These trees weren't here before. They're so tall."

Mary didn't know what to say. He reminded her of a movie she saw once, where coma patients wake up and they don't recognize anything. Or *The Shawshank Redemption*, where an old man got out of jail after decades and decades of being locked up and he didn't understand how the world worked anymore. She was pretty sure that character ended up killing himself.

"I'll be back tomorrow. Just . . . just stay here, okay?"

John nodded and began to drift among the trees, looking around. Mary could barely see his feet move—he just seemed to float, like a twig caught in a stream.

Mary watched him for a while longer. She wondered whether she was doing the right

thing. When she walked away, he was still looking out toward where the trees thinned and you could see all the way to the water.